KU-093-794

for Colin and Hilary

MYRIAD BOOKS LIMITED
35 Bishopsthorpe Road, London SE26 4PA

First published in 1998 by
ANDERSEN PRESS LTD
20 Vauxhall Bridge Road,
London SW1V 2SA

Published in Australia by Random House Australia Pty.,
20 Alfred Street, Milsons Point, Sydney, NSW 2061

Text and illustrations copyright © Ruth Brown, 1998

The rights of Ruth Brown to be identified as the author and illustrator of this
work have been asserted by her in accordance with the Copyright, Designs and
Patents Act, 1988.

All rights reserved. No part of this publication may be reproduced, stored in a
retrieval system, or transmitted, in any form or by any means electronic, mechani-
cal, photocopying or otherwise, without prior permission of the copyright owner.

ISBN 1 905606 10 9

Printed in China

Ruth Brown's
Mad Summer Night's Dream

written and illustrated by
Ruth Brown

MYRIAD BOOKS LIMITED

It was midsummer night in winter
and snow was on the ground,

When miles away, inside my head,
I heard an eerie sound.

I went down to the cellar
to look from an upstairs room,

The flowers were singing sweetly,
the birds were in full bloom.

Quite clearly in the distance,
but almost out of sight,

two fat cats were yowling,
preparing for a fight.

They were staring at each other
while sitting back to back.
One was black with brown stripes,
the brown one's stripes were black.

Three stone monkeys sprang to life,
and danced around with glee.
The blind one said, "I volunteer
to be the referee."
He said he'd watch the hissing cats
to supervise fair play —
The silent monkey by his side
said, "That will be the day!"
The other monkey next to him
said he would keep the score,
for though he couldn't hear a thing,
he'd heard it all before.

But as they started fighting
the wall came tumbling down;

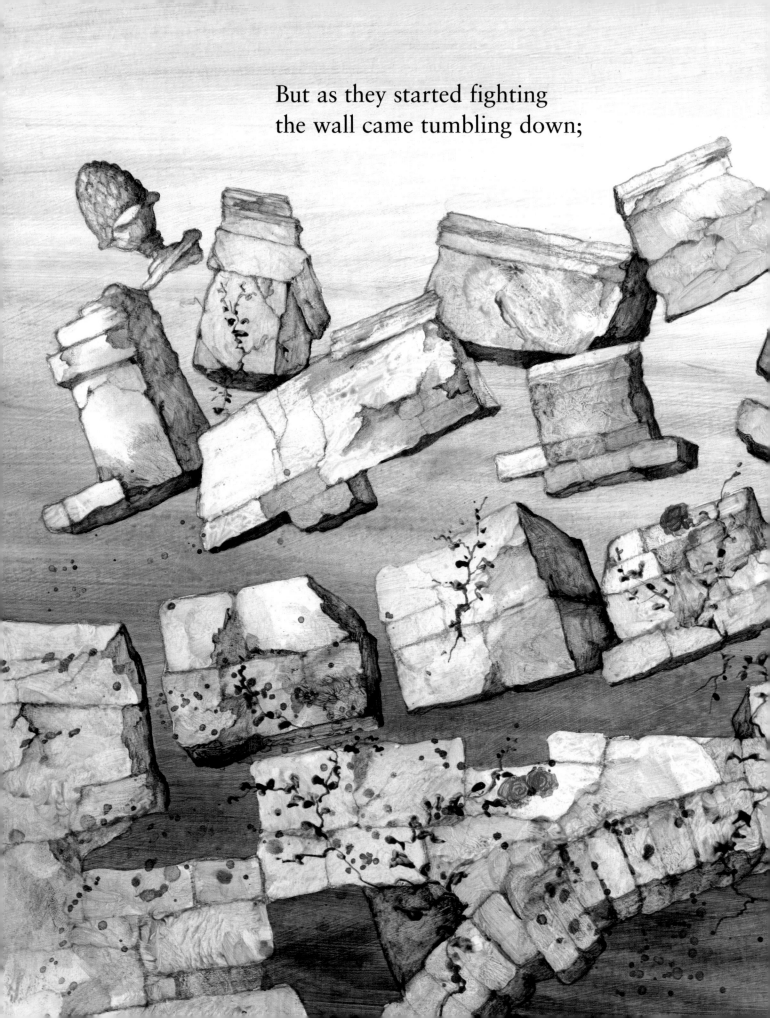

The cats fell into a dried–up ditch —
I thought that they would drown.

I jumped straight in to save them,
and heard a piercing scream...

It woke me up —

— it was morning!
What a mad midsummer night's dream.